ELBERT
the Mind Reader

by BARBARA RINKOFF

Illustrated by Paul Galdone

SCHOLASTIC BOOK SERVICES

NEW YORK • TORONTO • LONDON • AUCKLAND • SYDNEY

To Herb, with love

Text Copyright © 1967 by Barbara Rinkoff. Illustrations Copyright © 1967 by Lothrop, Lee & Shepard Co., Inc. This edition is published by Scholastic Book Services, a division of Scholastic Magazines, Inc., by arrangement with Lothrop, Lee & Shepard Co., Inc.

1st printing .... September 1968

Printed in the U.S.A.

Contents

Rejected

Elbert Hugo Berry III strode across the school grounds toward the football field. He was full of hope. Team tryout day for ninth-graders had finally arrived. He checked his watch. There was plenty of time to report to Coach and still make his yearly dental checkup on time. Of all days for his mother to arrange an appointment, Elbert thought; today was the worst. He certainly didn't want to rush Coach in any way.

Elbert heard his name being called. He turned and saw Scott sprinting after him.

"Hey, wait up," his classmate called. "You heading for the field? Trying out for the team?" he asked skeptically.

"Yup," Elbert answered. He looked Scott over. "Guess you'll have no trouble getting on the team."

Scott grinned. "Guess not," he admitted. "Hope *you* make it."

Elbert crossed his fingers. Ever since he could remember he had loved football. When his friends were small they had lugged around toy cars, baseball mitts, or guns, but he had always carried a football. He came by it naturally enough. His father had played football in high school and at college. For as long as Elbert could recall, Mr. Berry had patiently answered his questions and briefed him on plays. Elbert memorized all the information he could get, and he knew football inside out, but it hadn't paid off yet.

All through elementary school he had played whenever his friends did. But by eighth grade it was obvious to Elbert that when a game was set up at recess or after school, no one picked him for any team. Oh, they would admit that he knew the rules better than anyone, and that he could run and pass and kick fairly well, but they also realized that almost any of the other team members had no trouble flattening him as soon as they overtook him. And it was true. Mentally Elbert was a football giant, but physically he was on the frail side — small and spindly. If only he weighed more, or could run so fast that no one could catch him, they said.

All summer long Elbert ate and ran, and ran and ate. But the two seemed to cancel out each other. He tried devoting all his efforts to running, but that alone didn't help — he lost weight. When he concentrated on eating, he wasn't hungry enough to eat much without the exercise of running. When he did both, neither worked. He kept at practicing kicking, passing, and catching at every opportunity. But what he pinned his hopes on was that he had grown two inches. "I'm bigger," he consoled himself. "When I try out, that will help."

As the boys joined the group in front of Coach they took their places in the lineup. Elbert was a little dismayed to see the other tryouts assembled on the field. He knew most of them. The same boys that had been knocking him flat in elementary school. Elbert watched Coach size up the players and go for the husky ones. But he did pick Jim, and Jim was as skinny as Elbert was. Elbert looked down at his shoulders. He'd have to admit, though, that both of his own could fit on one side of Jim's. Elbert stood up as straight as he could, hoping he looked broader.

Coach worked at a businesslike pace setting up the team, and before Elbert could grow impatient Coach was before him. "Well, son, what can I do for you?" he inquired.

Elbert swallowed hard. "I'm going out for the team," he heard his voice respond.

Coach stroked his chin and shook his head. "Come back when you've filled out and grown some," he advised.

Elbert took a step forward and breathed deeply to expand his chest. "I may look . . . uh . . . a little smaller than they are, but I can pass and run, and I know the rules by heart. Gee, Coach, let me try."

Coach frowned and patted Elbert on the shoulder. "Sorry, son, those fellows would make mincemeat out of you on the field. I couldn't take the chance."

"But . . . I'm fast . . ." Elbert's voice trailed off.

"Not a chance, son. Another year . . ."

Elbert bit his lip. He wanted to tell Coach to think it over, not to rush into a decision, but he knew a NO when he heard it.

Coach watched Elbert struggle. "Well, son, if you want to be with the team so much, you can be water boy," he offered.

Elbert shook his head. He didn't want that job. It was the team or . . . or nothing. Slowly he turned on his heel and made his way across the practice field.

Down the road he plodded, head lowered, hands

dug deep in his pockets, kicking at the stones as he went. He remembered his dental appointment, consulted his watch, and forced himself to walk a little faster. He really didn't feel much like seeing anyone, but if it had to be someone, Dr. Shaw wasn't bad. In fact, Elbert never minded his yearly visits. The dentist usually took X rays and cleaned his teeth, and he told jokes as he worked. There were times Elbert wished he had to go more often — not for dental care, but to hear the stories. He just hoped Dr. Shaw wouldn't mention anything about football today. He couldn't stand that.

Elbert walked up the steps onto Dr. Shaw's front porch. The bell tinkled as he entered, and he picked up a magazine to thumb through as he took a seat in the reception room. It was hard to concentrate on reading. He kept hearing Coach's NO echoing in his ears.

It wasn't long before Miss Booth, the dental assistant, ushered him into the treatment room, settled him in the dental chair, pumped it up, and arranged a towel at his neck.

"Well, hello, Elbert," Dr. Shaw boomed as he came into the room. He took some X rays and began cleaning Elbert's teeth as Miss Booth developed the pictures. Elbert was unusually quiet throughout.

Dr. Shaw eyed him curiously. "Why so glum?" he asked.

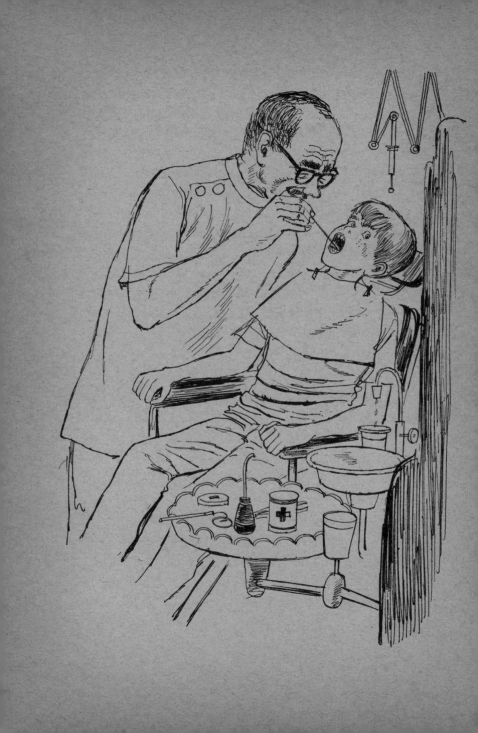

Elbert looked down at the footrest.

"Can't be school marks . . . not you," Dr. Shaw observed. "By the way, how's the football?"

Elbert looked at the ceiling and then out of the window.

"So that's the trouble. Haven't made the team yet, eh? Don't give up . . . one of these days . . . now open wide and let's have a look."

Elbert leaned back and opened obediently.

"Mmmmmmmm. Ah ha! Looks as though we have a little work today, Elbert." Dr. Shaw poked around with the explorer and Elbert could feel it hooking into something. "Yes sir, you have a cavity this time." He checked the X rays. "Not too bad though. We can fill it right now." As he worked he hummed the tune that the office radio was playing.

Elbert settled back and watched Dr. Shaw get ready to fix his tooth. With the new drill it didn't take long to prepare the cavity, and before he knew it Miss Booth was mixing a filling.

"Going to use a new alloy on this," Dr. Shaw was saying. "Makes a good tight filling, sets quickly, and we can polish it right away."

Elbert's mouth was stuffed with a cotton roll and he didn't feel much like talking anyway, so he sat quietly brooding over his disappointment. Dr. Shaw hadn't even told any jokes. All he had done was keep humming slightly off tune to the radio which

11

was piped throughout the entire office. Nothing at all was going right today.

Dr. Shaw removed the cotton roll, waited a moment, and then polished the surface of the filling. "Well now, that's that," he said, leaving the chair and moving into the next room. "See you in six months this time. Regards to your mother," he called over his shoulder. Miss Booth removed the towel, lowered the chair, said good-bye to Elbert, and went to join the dentist and the next patient.

Elbert ran his tongue over the metal in his tooth. It felt slick and cool. He took a drink of water from the paper cup and started to leave the room when a sudden blast of static rattled his head. "That's some powerful radio the doctor has," he thought.

In a moment the static cleared and the sound of music hummed low in his ears. Then he listened more closely. Two different songs seemed to be playing at the same time. It was worse than Dr. Shaw's off-key humming. Must be two stations interfering with each other, Elbert thought, and he hurried out to escape the conflicting noises.

He passed Dr. Shaw and Miss Booth working in the next treatment room, and went by the dentist's consultation room and out the door into the reception room. A large woman with a baby on her lap was sitting there. As soon as the child spotted Elbert he began to wail.

Between the static, the confusing music, and the crying of the baby in his ears, Elbert could hardly wait to leave Dr. Shaw's office. It was bedlam in there. He didn't know how anyone could stand it. Out the door he went and down the front porch steps.

Something strange was going on, though. He could no longer hear the baby crying, and one song had stopped abruptly as soon as he closed Dr. Shaw's front door. But the other song was going right along with him!

An Amazing Discovery

Elbert stood on the sidewalk in front of the dentist's office. He ran his tongue over his lips and swallowed. The faint crackle of static buzzed in his ears, and he heard an interruption of the program. He worked his jaw and was startled when the music went off and on. It sounded exactly the same way it did when he used to clap his hands tightly over his ears for fun and then release them suddenly. He frowned and gritted his teeth, and immediately the music boomed so loud in his head that his jaw automatically fell open. And the moment it did, there was silence.

Elbert wanted badly to swallow, but to tell the truth, he was afraid to close his mouth. Then, very carefully, he began to close his teeth together, and sure enough, it started again. First the static, then the soft sound of music began. The tighter he clenched his teeth, the louder it played. In a way it was really funny. Imagine having a built-in radio! That new stuff Dr. Shaw put in his tooth must be acting like a receiver.

He tried moving his jaw with his teeth touching, and the music changed. Now a soap opera was playing loud and clear in his head. Gingerly he moved his jaw again. Each time he changed the position of his teeth another station tuned in. Elbert shook his head in disbelief. Once more he wiggled his mouth. Yes sir, that was the way to tune. Not only was he a walking radio, but he knew how to control it. He could turn it on and off, change stations, and make it louder or softer.

"What a gift," he thought to himself. "Wait till I tell Mom and Dad, and the kids at school. When I don't like what the teacher's teaching, I can just turn on my radio and listen to that instead. And at bedtime I can listen to it all night long if I want to. No one can make me turn it off."

Elbert was walking quickly toward home when an awful thought came to him. "If I tell Mom and Dad about my radio, they'll make Dr. Shaw change that filling. Then I won't have it any more." Elbert wasn't about to give up this great thing that had happened to him, and that meant he couldn't tell anyone about it. He stood quietly for a moment and then continued on home.

Mrs. Berry was knitting in the living room when Elbert came in.

"Been to Dr. Shaw's?" she asked.

"Yup. Sends regards to you," Elbert answered, being careful to keep his teeth apart when his mouth was closed. "I had a cavity this time," he continued in a low voice.

"Oh, really?" his mother answered. "Not brushing them clean enough," she added, nodding vigorously. "Did you have time to try out for the football team first?"

"Mmmmmm," Elbert replied.

"And?" his mother insisted on asking.

"No soap . . . too small."

"What a shame, dear. Maybe next year . . ."

Elbert stopped listening. He walked to the kitchen, with her following. There were some freshly baked cupcakes cooling on the table. "May I have some?" he asked.

His mother felt the cakes. "They're still a little warm. All right, just two," she said. "And don't forget to brush your teeth afterward."

Elbert settled himself at the table, while Mrs. Berry busied herself at the stove. He attacked the first cupcake. It was rather peculiar hearing a flash of music each time his teeth touched. He wished that he could let his mother in on the secret. He was bursting to tell someone.

Bong, bong, bong, sounded the hourly newscast on his radio. Elbert listened intermittently as the world and then the local news came to him between bites. He wasn't too interested in that. But when the local sportscaster started his report, Elbert stopped eating his cake, and his ears pricked up at the mention of his school.

"The freshman team of Rivertown High will have a tough time beating Sampson High this year. Unless they can develop a good quarterback who can analyze the plays and come up with . . ."

"What's wrong, dear? Don't you like the cupcakes?" Mrs. Berry's voice drowned out the radio.

"Sh . . . don't interrupt this," Elbert answered unthinkingly.

"Interrupt what, dear?"

Elbert focused on his mother standing before him. He shifted uneasily on his chair. "Interrupt . . . uh . . . interrupt this idea about some schoolwork I was thinking about," he stammered.

"Oh," Mrs. Berry murmured.

Elbert drew a deep breath. That nearly did it, he thought. He'd better be more careful after this. He

closed his teeth and listened again. The news was over. He rose from the table, and his mother again reminded him to brush his teeth. He shook his head and rolled his eyes, but moved to the bathroom to carry out her orders. He wondered what effect toothpaste and brushing might have on his radio.

When he was before the mirror above the bathroom sink, he inspected the new filling carefully. It gleamed smoothly, and Elbert could almost swear that it threw off little silvery sparks. He brushed it till it shone like nothing he had ever seen before. He was quite pleased with himself as he went to join his mother, who had gone back to her knitting in the living room.

"Did you brush?" she asked.

"Uh huh," he answered and sat down with a thump on the sofa next to her.

"Poor dear . . . disappointed again."

Elbert looked sharply at his mother. He was sure he'd heard her speak, yet her mouth was closed and she was busy over her knitting.

"Too bad his heart's so set on that team. I must tell Bert not to make too much of it tonight."

Elbert stared hard. His mother's lips were not moving and her eyes were on her work. He cleared his throat. "Did you . . . uh . . . say something, Mom?" he asked, his voice sounding strange to his ears.

Mrs. Berry looked searchingly at his face. "No, dear," she said, "not a thing."

Elbert ran his tongue around his dry lips.

"Poor child's overwrought. Such a disappointment after trying so hard . . ."

Elbert swallowed hard. He had heard it again. Brushing his teeth had affected his new filling — now he could hear what people were thinking!

Sharing the Secret

ELBERT SAT RIGIDLY next to his mother. It seemed almost impossible that he could hear her think. But he had — three times! He disengaged his teeth, and the resulting quiet made his head feel empty and light. "Am I going to hear people think from now on?" he wondered. Very carefully he closed his jaw. The teeth were touching again, but Mrs. Berry was no longer coming in clearly. Very faintly Elbert could just about make out her thoughts.

"Seven more stitches to this line. One, two, three . . ." Mrs. Berry's thoughts faded out completely.

Elbert strained closer, but he couldn't hear a thing. He got up and moved away from the sofa.

He needed to be alone to think things out. Mrs. Berry was so absorbed in her counting that she merely nodded when Elbert said that he was going to his room. He proceeded down the hall and up the staircase with a heavy step, concentrating all his efforts on keeping his mouth closed and his teeth apart.

Elbert pushed open his door and looked around the room. The twin bed stood in its usual place against the wall. There was the dresser, and his desk with the chair shoved tightly into the kneehole stood beneath the window. Yes, everything was as it had always been — everything, that is, except Elbert.

He moved in front of his dresser, looked into the mirror which hung above it, and studied himself closely. The same small face greeted his dark-brown eyes. And there was the reddish-brown straight hair flopping down across his forehead. He wrinkled his snub nose with the mass of freckles across it, and his cheeks rode up and down. Same old face as always. He squinted into the mirror and then turned away. Anyone looking at him could never tell that he was different, but Elbert had a feeling that from now on nothing would be the same.

More than ever he wished he could talk to someone about it — but who? If only he had a brother or sister, he could tell them and they wouldn't snitch. But Elbert was an only child. Maybe he could tell Dusty North. Dusty was his best friend — his classmate and neighbor. They often shared secrets. But then Elbert had never had a secret like this one before. He wasn't quite sure how Dusty would take it. Still, why not give it a try? He just had to tell somebody. Elbert turned on his heel and marched determinedly out of the room and down the stairs.

"Going over to Dusty's," he called to his mother, and the slam of the back door almost drowned out her "Don't be late for supper."

Elbert strode across the back lawn toward Dusty's house. He couldn't make up his mind whether he was happy or sad about his new ability. The radio business was strange enough, but hearing people's thoughts was another matter entirely! A fellow could get into a lot of trouble with that . . . but then, maybe it could be lots of fun, too.

Dusty was sitting on his back porch steps, stuffing a banana into his mouth with one hand and flexing the muscles of the other arm at the same time. Elbert admired his husky frame. He wished he had such wide shoulders, and muscles that bulged.

"Hi, Dust," he called.

Dusty nodded, not missing a bite. He gulped down his mouthful and turned his full attention to Elbert. "Did you make the team?" he asked.

Elbert scowled. "Nope, same old excuse," he muttered.

"Tough. To tell the truth, I didn't think you would. Not enough here." Dusty pounded his hulking chest.

Elbert looked at his shoes. One thing about Dusty, he was frank. Sometimes Elbert wished that he weren't. But no matter how blunt Dusty was, he was a pal, and he did toss the football with him even when none of the other guys would.

"Didn't see you at the tryouts," Elbert remarked.

"Coach said never mind coming. He's seen me play. I'm on the team automatically."

Elbert nodded. "It figures," he said aloud, and he sat down next to Dusty.

"Have some fruit?" Dusty offered, pointing to a dish on the steps near him.

Elbert took a slice of apple and wondered how he could turn the talk to his new discovery. Should he come right out and say that he was a walking radio? And what about hearing people think? He leaned toward Dusty and listened hard, wondering if he could pick up anything. Only a faint buzz was coming through. He figured that something about brushing his new filling made it sensitive to thought waves. Judging from what had happened with his mother, the power lasted only for a short time. He was anxious to brush again to test whether it would work every time, but of course he would look mighty silly sitting out here in public brushing his tooth! He could see that Dusty was looking at him rather peculiarly.

"What's eating you?" Dusty asked.

Elbert cleared his throat. He wanted to tell and here was his chance. But how? He thought a moment. Maybe it would work. "Hey, bring out your transistor. I'll show you something," he answered.

"What?" Dusty asked skeptically.

"Get it . . . you'll see."

Dusty left to return shortly with the transistor. "What's to see?" he asked.

"Bet I can tell you what's on any of the stations," Elbert answered. He ground his teeth together to stir up the filling.

"Huh!" Dusty snorted. "Go on."

Elbert set his jaw, working it around again until one station came in clearly. Then he listened. "Bet one of 'em is playing 'Gee Whiz Baby,'" he said.

Dusty snapped on the transistor and twirled the dial. "Well, I'll be . . ." he muttered. "How'd you know?" Then his face lit up and he lowered his voice to a more confidential tone. "What's the trick? Come on, let me in on it."

Elbert grinned. "It's no trick . . . not really," he answered.

"Yeah? Then what is it?" Dusty asked. "Let's see you do it again."

Elbert worked his jaw again and concentrated. Finally he spoke. "Another station has a man talking about air pollution."

Dusty spun the dial again. "Come on, now, what's going on?" he asked. "How'd you know? We always share our secrets, don't we? Let me in on it."

Elbert cleared his throat again and spoke in a low voice. "I went to Dr. Shaw's office today and the filling he put in my tooth acts like a radio receiver." Elbert paused to see the effect.

Dusty eyed him up and down and then spoke slowly. "You serious, Elbert? You're kidding me — you don't want to tell. You learned some kind of trick and you're holding out."

"No, honestly . . ."

"You don't fool me," Dusty cut in. "You're mad because you didn't make the team, so you're getting even."

"But, Dusty, it's true," Elbert protested.

"Sure, sure. I never heard of fillings that were radios — at least not for real. Come on, give it to me straight."

Elbert raised his right hand high in the air. "Honest, it's the truth. Ever since I got that filling put in, things have been happening."

Dusty stroked his chin, weighing Elbert's words.

After a long silence Dusty shrugged. "You're really not kidding me, are you?" he asked, more as a statement than as a question.

Elbert drew a deep breath. "I swear," he declared.

"Let me hear it," Dusty demanded. He moved closer to Elbert and cocked his head to listen. "I don't hear anything. Is it playing now?"

Elbert clamped his jaw and nodded.

Dusty leaned over and put his ear to Elbert's cheek, frowning in concentration.

Elbert shifted uncomfortably. "You hear it now?" he asked.

Dusty sat up, wiggling his finger vigorously in his ear. "Not really — maybe just a faint hum," he admitted.

"Try it this way." Elbert kept his teeth shut but opened his lips as widely as he could manage.

Dusty put his ear to Elbert's mouth and listened intently. "I hear something," he shouted, bobbing his head up suddenly and ramming smack into Elbert's nose.

"Ouch," yelled Elbert, grabbing his nose.

"Sorry," Dusty said quickly, "I'd better be careful. Who knows, your nose might be the antenna."

Elbert smiled weakly. "Well, what do you think?" he asked, rubbing his nose tenderly.

Dusty's eyebrows shot up and his face lit with a

broad smile. "I think you've got it made, Elbert," he shouted. "Boy, if I had that filling I could listen to them broadcast my own plays in the Saturday games. And when my dad lectured me about school marks I could tune in some station and drown him out. What a deal!"

Elbert folded his arms casually across his chest and smiled. "And that's not all," he said.

"Heck no. It's got thousands of possibilities," Dusty agreed.

Elbert leaned a little closer. "I mean I can do something even more terrific."

"What?" Dusty demanded.

Elbert cleared his throat and his eyebrows drew together. "I can hear what people think," he said softly.

Dusty blinked in a dazed fashion. "No kidding!" he sputtered.

Elbert nodded solemnly.

Dusty's mouth had dropped open and his head wagged back and forth. When he was able to talk all that came out was, *Holy cow!* Finally he added in an awed tone, "Can I see you do it?"

Elbert frowned. "I can only pick up thought waves when I brush the filling and really sensitize it."

"You mean you need to walk around with tooth-paste and a toothbrush?"

"Seems that way," Elbert admitted, and proceeded to tell Dusty about the experience with his mother.

"Are you sure that it works every time? Let's test it, okay?" Dusty asked anxiously. He stood up quickly and started indoors. "I'll get you the stuff," he called over his shoulder.

Elbert settled in a comfortable position, spread a blob of paste on the toothbrush, and ran it over his new filling. At first he used gentle strokes, and then he attacked it vigorously. He foamed at the mouth from the paste, but ignored it. Sitting back, he closed his eyes, worked his jaw, and concentrated.

Dusty leaned over him, breathing down his neck. "Anything coming in yet?" he asked.

Elbert cocked his head, wiped his mouth off on his sleeve, and held his finger up for silence. Dusty fidgeted impatiently, never taking his eyes off Elbert. And then through clenched teeth, came Elbert's voice. "If you want me to demonstrate you'd better start thinking of something else besides 'Come on . . . come on . . . what do you hear?'"

Dusty's head bobbed vigorously. "That's what I'm thinking . . . it sure is," he roared.

"Well, come up with something more interesting than that."

"Heck, I'm so excited that my mind's a blank. What should I think about?"

"If I tell you what to think about, that won't be any test of my powers. You'll have to think of something by yourself. Shhh . . . something's coming in. Let me make it louder." Elbert readjusted his bite, listened, and then reported. "Fruit's gone again! Some day that boy will turn into a fruit salad. Where is he? He'd better get to his homework, or no more football!"

"Oh boy, that's not me coming in. That's my mom," Dusty groaned.

"Yup. Sounds like her," Elbert agreed.

"I'll be in to do my homework in a second, Mom," Dusty called just as his mother poked her head out of the back door.

"I see you know what I'm thinking," she declared.

Dusty and Elbert exchanged knowing glances.

"Ought to by now," Mrs. North added.

Elbert bristled. Her remark had squelched him a little. The boys waited until she closed the door before they started to talk again.

"What do you think I ought to do?" Elbert asked.

Dusty slapped his thigh. "Do? I'd say you could do just about anything, old pal. Be a spy for the FBI, get up a circus act . . ."

"I mean, should I let my folks know and take the chance that maybe they'll tell Dr. Shaw to change my filling, or should I keep it a secret?"

Dusty stuck out his lower lip and considered the problem. "You can't take chances. It'll have to be a secret. You don't want to give up a deal like this, do you?" he asked.

Elbert's head shook vigorously. He was glad that Dusty had seconded his own private opinion.

"Wait till school tomorrow . . . will we have fun!" Dusty picked up the fruit plate and started indoors. "Don't forget to bring your toothbrush and paste. I'd better get at the old homework before Mom blows a fuse. The team needs me! See you tomorrow — and take good care of that filling!"

Dinner was just about over by the time Mrs. Berry steered the conversation around to Elbert's day. Until then his father had been so busy telling them about a new business deal that Elbert thought he might escape having to be there when his dad heard the news about his not making the team. In fact, Elbert was just scraping back his chair to leave the table when Mrs. Berry told about the visit to the dentist and then, ever so casually, mentioned about the football team. Elbert could see her give his father the high sign, so that he wouldn't make too much of it.

Mr. Berry flushed and began to fold his table napkin with special care. "Too bad, son," he murmured. Then in a forced jovial voice he added, "Well, we can't win them all, eh?"

Elbert looked at his shoes.

Mrs. Berry smiled protectively at him. "Don't forget to brush your teeth after eating," she said, trying to change the subject.

Elbert nodded, anxious to escape for any reason. He went up to the bathroom quickly. He knew how much of a disappointment it was to his dad to have him rejected for the team. And remembering the whole scene again made him feel low. Without thinking he took his toothbrush and began to brush.

Elbert hadn't been in the bathroom more than a minute when Mr. Berry popped his head in. He looked at Elbert and smiled. "Don't take it too hard, son, maybe one of these days . . ." His voice trailed off and he disappeared into the hallway.

Elbert put down the brush and gritted his teeth. He wished that no one would mention the incident again. A sudden loud sound rocked his head. He moved his jaw carefully, fine-tuning it in.

"Darn shame they don't give the kid a chance. Why, he could outplay them all. He knows the game inside out. All he needs is a chance to show them."

Elbert relaxed his jaw so that he wouldn't hear his

father any more. He wished that he *could* have a chance to show Coach. He looked down and saw the toothbrush on the sink. There was nothing on it. He had forgotten to use toothpaste.

Elbert scratched his head. Gee, he could tune into other people's thoughts with just the brush. That was great . . . that would be easier . . . that would be . . . A slow grin began to light his face.

Trouble in School

ELBERT SLIPPED INTO HIS SEAT in social studies class just before the bell rang. He had been listening to his radio so intently all morning that he forgot to leave for school on time and had missed walking with Dusty. He tapped his jacket pocket to feel for the toothbrush. It was there all right, safe and sound. Elbert swiveled around in his seat to give Dusty the high sign, and as he did, Mrs. McGovern stood up at her desk and called the class to order. Elbert was only able to catch a glimpse of Dusty frantically pretending to brush his teeth before he had to turn around again.

Elbert longed to close his teeth and listen to something more interesting than the teacher's voice droning on and on in a flat tone about the time of

Charlemagne. After a while it was more than he could resist. He tightened his jaw, gritted his teeth, and began to concentrate on the program coming in.

It was a panel discussion on whether or not high school students were receiving too much homework these days. Elbert heartily agreed with one educator when he stated that homework could be instructional, but that too much busy work was assigned by many teachers instead. He sat nodding solemnly in his seat. Then another panelist announced that, as a mother, she felt that her child was not assigned enough work because she often came home with none. Elbert gripped the edges of his desk and his eyes narrowed. He felt strongly about the subject.

"And what is your opinion on this matter, Elbert?"

He heard his name called out and jumped to his feet. "I think if it's to teach something, it's a good idea, but otherwise it's a waste of time."

"Well!" Mrs. McGovern exploded. "I hardly think that it occurred for the purpose of teaching us something, nor can we look upon the event as a waste of time!"

Elbert blinked and groaned to himself. He hadn't the vaguest idea what she was talking about.

"Class, please repeat the question for Elbert's benefit," the teacher snapped.

"Why do you think Charlemagne's empire broke up?" the class intoned.

Elbert felt himself getting red. Out of the corner of his eye he could see Dusty clutching his head.

After a long and uncomfortable silence Mrs. McGovern cleared her throat. "You had better pay attention, Elbert. Sit down," she said and turned her attention to the discussion of the question.

Elbert ran his tongue around his dry lips and lowered himself into his seat. It was the second time today that he had been carried away by his radio and had gotten himself into difficulties. Elbert forced his tongue between his teeth. He was in enough trouble already. He had to be more careful.

As the class went on, Elbert tried desperately to pay attention to the discussion. It wasn't easy. He had to remind himself to keep his teeth from making contact. It was difficult to remember to do that and to keep his mind on social studies at the same time.

Mrs. McGovern had gotten into a long, involved debate with one of the more interested students. The subject didn't appeal much to Elbert, and little by little he found himself drifting off, thinking about his radio. The teacher was so occupied that Elbert decided it wouldn't hurt any if he tuned in for a second — just to hear what was on. After all, who would know? He took another quick look at Mrs. McGovern and then carefully gritted his teeth.

Ever so faintly he began to get reception. A waltz floated through his head. He didn't care much for that. Elbert readjusted his jaw. He wasn't going to bother to listen to a soap commercial. Again he tuned. This time it was a political discussion. Elbert listened. They were talking about whether to re-elect the present town mayor or to vote for his opponent. Elbert liked the mayor, Mr. Rogers. The other guy had a mean face and was telling people he'd do all sorts of things that Mr. Berry said were ridiculous campaign promises. Elbert shook his head, agreeing with the man speaking in favor of the mayor.

Suddenly Elbert heard his name being called again. He let his jaw go slack and struggled to his feet. Mrs. McGovern smiled at him.

"And how do you vote?" she asked.

"For Mr. Rogers," Elbert answered in a clear voice.

The teacher's face reddened. "For Mr. Rogers?" she repeated.

"Yes, ma'am."

"Do you really think that he'd want to be the chairman of our class clean-up squad?"

The girls began to giggle, and then the throaty laughter of the boys drowned them out.

Elbert blinked. He had really made a fool of himself this time. Without thinking, his hand went up to his jaw and a pained expression crossed his face.

"Do you have a toothache?" Mrs. McGovern asked.

Elbert's hand fell and he shook his head. Toothache nothing — what he had was a headache!

The teacher rapped for silence. "I would like to see you after class, Elbert," she announced.

Elbert turned and sank into his seat. He could see all the kids looking at him as if he were crazy. Dusty was shaking his head sadly. Elbert wished that he could sink into the floor.

When class was dismissed, Mrs. McGovern motioned Elbert to her desk. He moved up the aisle, feeling her eyes upon him.

"Whatever has gotten into you, Elbert?" she asked.

Elbert swallowed hard. He could hardly say, "A radio has gotten into me, ma'am," so he didn't say anything.

The teacher's eyebrows drew together in a worried frown. "If you won't explain, I'm afraid that I shall have to ask you to report here after school for detention."

Elbert looked at his shoes and remained silent.

"Well," Mrs. McGovern declared, "be here after school. I'll deal with you then."

Elbert dug his hands into his pockets and made his way out of the classroom.

At lunchtime he finally had time to explain to Dusty what had happened.

"Gee," his friend sympathized, "what a mess you've gotten into."

Elbert couldn't have agreed more. "What do you think I should do?" he asked.

Dusty looked at him silently through half-closed eyes. "Maybe you ought to try to hear what she's thinking when you report after school," he said. "Then you can find out if you can do or say anything that would make her forget the whole thing."

"What an idea!" Elbert exploded. "Of course — why didn't I think of it?"

"Don't forget to brush your tooth before you see her."

"Heck no," Elbert replied as he tapped the toothbrush in his pocket.

When the final bell of the afternoon sounded, Elbert sprinted down the hall from his last class to his locker. He gathered his things quickly and started toward the bathroom for a quick brushing session. As he moved down the hall he left the sudden pressure of a hand gripping his shoulder.

"You haven't forgotten our appointment, have you?" a voice inquired. Elbert didn't need to look around to know that it was Mrs. McGovern.

"No ma'am," he declared, "I was just . . ."

"On your way to my room. Fine, we can go together then." She fell into step beside him.

Elbert felt as if he were a prisoner being marched off to the firing squad.

"You may sit at your desk, Elbert, and think," the teacher announced as they entered her classroom.

"Think about what?" Elbert wondered as he lowered himself into the seat. Was he supposed to concentrate on Charlemagne — or the chairman for the class clean-up squad? Out of the corner of his eye Elbert watched Mrs. McGovern settle herself at her desk and begin working over some papers. Moving as cautiously as he was able, he began to inch the toothbrush out of his pocket. He managed to get it free and had just about put it into his mouth when the teacher looked up, straight at him. Elbert jammed the brush further into his mouth, and his hand flew up to cover the protruding handle.

"I'm glad to see you looking concerned," his teacher said, and then returned her gaze to her work.

Elbert groaned to himself. The toothbrush was rammed so far back in his throat that he could almost have brushed his tonsils. He'd have to work fast. With one eye on Mrs. McGovern, Elbert ran the brush vigorously back and forth over his filling. Then quickly he returned the toothbrush to his pocket and concentrated all his efforts on clenching his teeth and getting the teacher's thoughts tuned in.

At first the signal was weak, but within seconds he could hear it loud and clear.

"Peculiar boy . . . always seemed so sensible, and now . . . oh well, just another few papers to go and I can leave for my appointment with the chiropodist. That corn is killing me. It's a wonder I made it through the day."

Elbert was about to feel sorry for her when another thought wave interrupted.

"Look at him sitting there. You'd think that he'd have the brains to apologize instead of waiting for me to reprimand him again."

Elbert relaxed his jaw abruptly, and the teacher's thoughts faded immediately. His hand shot up and waved frantically.

After a long moment Mrs. McGovern looked up. "Yes?" she asked.

Elbert rose from his seat and faced the teacher. "I would like to apologize for not paying attention in class today," he said solemnly.

Mrs. McGovern studied him silently, and then her face relaxed into a slow smile.

"That's better," she said. "After this you must remember to keep your thoughts tuned to class. You can go now."

Elbert nodded vigorously. He picked up his things and scurried out of the room. Mrs. McGovern didn't dream how right she was about tuning, he thought, as he escaped into the afternoon sunlight.

Disappointment

ELBERT SHADED HIS EYES and looked across the school grounds toward the football practice field. The team was already in motion, performing the usual warm-up exercises. "Might as well watch them," he thought to himself. Then afterward he could walk home with Dusty and discuss the day's happenings.

As he approached he could see about twenty-five boys on the field. Coach was demonstrating stance to some of the players. When the whistle blew, the group knelt down into a three-point stance. Up and down they went while Coach gave them pointers about distributing their weight correctly. Another group of boys was busy grunting over push-ups, while still a third was running up and back the width of the field. Elbert settled down on the bottommost bench along the side of the field and watched the boys. They were all larger and heavier than he was. He was shaking his head mournfully when he noticed Coach walking toward him.

"I see you've decided to join us after all," Coach said. "As a matter of fact, I'm glad that you turned up today. I was going to send for you. I think maybe . . ." Coach was interrupted by one of the players on the field shouting to him for instructions on the next exercise.

"In a moment," Coach yelled back through cupped hands. Then turning again to Elbert he thrust something into his hands. "Here, take this stopwatch and start timing the runners. Keep a record of their time for me. I think that you'll make an excellent . . ." The boys on the field began calling again and Coach broke off midsentence. "I'll talk to you later," he said over his shoulder, leaving Elbert standing expectantly.

Elbert smiled. Maybe things were going to work out after all. Coach had said that he was going to send for him. He seemed to have something in mind. Maybe he had second thoughts about putting him on the team. Maybe he was going to give him a chance after all. Elbert threw back his head and sprinted toward the runners. He could see that one of them was Dusty.

"Hey, whatcha doing here?" Dusty called as he ran toward Elbert. "Joining the team?"

Elbert grinned, but didn't answer. Dusty looked at him quizzically, but Elbert ignored him. When the boys had circled around him he explained his mission. "Okay, Tom, Rick, Dusty, Jim, Bob, line up here. Pretend it's a race, and give me your best time," Elbert told them. He liked being involved in team practice; it felt every bit as good as he had thought it would. "Tell you what," he heard himself saying, "I'll run along with you — to pace you."

The boys laughed as they lined up. Elbert looked at the stopwatch. "Ready . . . set . . . go!" he roared, and broke with the others. Down the field he flew. All the practicing that he had done during the summer made his legs work automatically. He could hear the uneven thumps of his heart as he drew up across the finish line. He gave a quick look at his watch and turned to clock the other boys. He could see at a glance that he had been first. He made note of the time as the others came in.

"Whatcha trying to do . . . show us up?" Dusty panted as he came in with the others close at his heels.

"You're running even better than last year," Rick put in.

46

"It's that summer training he did," Dusty said.

"Thinks he's a quarterback," Tom grumbled.

Elbert grinned and ran his hand down the leg of his pants. He wished Coach had made that remark. Out of the corner of his eye he looked for Coach, only to find him with his back turned. Elbert was disappointed, but then, he reasoned, it wasn't important to impress Coach. After all, Coach already had some position in mind for him. He'd find out which later. "Okay, let's take it again," he said, giving the boys his full attention.

"Never mind pacing us," Jim answered. "We have enough troubles getting into shape without a speed demon running us ragged."

Elbert shrugged and started the countdown. Over and over he had the group practice fast breakaways and running back and forth. The time flew by so quickly that Elbert was surprised when Coach blew the whistle to signal the end of practice on the field.

"We'll have a skull session before showers," Coach announced. The group fell in, following the coach into the locker room.

Elbert cornered Coach as the boys took seats in a semicircle on benches in front of him.

"Got the figures?" Coach grunted.

Elbert reported his findings. Coach marked them down in a little black book and then turned to the boys. Elbert stood by uncertainly. He hated to make a pest of himself, but he did hope that Coach was ready to tell him what he had in mind for him. At first Coach didn't seem to notice that he was still standing there, but then as his glance fell on Elbert again he smiled.

"Take a seat, son," he said, "I'll speak with you later. Meanwhile listen carefully to these plays and see how much you can learn. It's important."

Elbert took off immediately for a seat next to Dusty, who was sitting at the rear of the group. He settled down contentedly. It was going to be great to be a part of the team. He grinned and poked Dusty in the ribs. Dusty elbowed him back, and then they both turned their attention to the blackboard that Coach had rolled out and was drawing on.

"Let's look at the Oklahoma 5-4 defensive alignment," Coach was saying as he made circles on the board.

Elbert recognized the formation from the many times that his father had briefed him on it.

Dusty leaned toward Elbert. "You out of trouble with McGovern?" he whispered.

Elbert quietly told him what had happened.

Dusty was pleased that his suggestion about listening to the teacher's thoughts had worked out well. "Try the toothbrush out on Coach," he urged. "Wonder what he thinks about while he's talking?"

Elbert decided that it might be fun. He ducked down, took out the brush, and gave his filling a vigorous workout. Almost at once his head began to reel from so many signals tuning in at the same time. Snatches of thought babbled at him, one overlapping the other. "When's he going to quit yapping? Hope the shower is hot. I've got a charley horse already! We'll never beat Sampson this year. My arms are killing me!" Elbert concentrated hard on Coach, trying to tune out the boys. It wasn't easy.

"Now think, boys: does that mean that for this type of play the Oklahoma defense will always work?" Coach was asking.

Some boys were nodding "Yes," others muttered "Uh huh," while some shrugged and weakly voiced their "I guess so."

Elbert knew the answer from his father's having drilled it into him, but he was too busy fine-tuning into Coach's thoughts to answer. "Clunkheads," Coach was thinking, "If I stand here and smile at them, they think the answer is 'Yes.' What this team needs is someone who can think."

Elbert realized at once that opportunity was knocking. He popped up from the bench so suddenly that he nearly knocked Dusty off balance. "I can!" he shouted.

"You can what?" Coach asked with a puzzled frown.

"I can think," Elbert answered, carried away with his own thoughts. Then feeling Coach's gaze upon him, he flushed. "I . . . I mean . . . I think it would be okay only if there were no change in wind," he stammered out the answer.

Coach's eyes lit up, and the boys swiveled around in their seats to look at Elbert.

Coach stroked his chin and eyed Elbert thoughtfully from head to toe. "That's correct," he grunted.

Elbert was so excited that he couldn't keep Coach tuned in. Anyway, he knew by just looking at Coach's expression that he was impressed. Elbert sat down feeling very satisfied with himself. As soon as the session was over, Coach would offer him the quarterback position straight off. But Elbert decided not to be a pig. If necessary he'd take any position to start. He was sure that after seeing him in action Coach would be happy to give him the place on the team that he had always wanted.

When the session broke up, Coach motioned Elbert toward him.

"Good reasoning there, Elbert," Coach greeted him. "You've demonstrated on the field today that you can work well. And just now you've shown that you can think. Those qualities are of great value to a team. As I mentioned earlier, I've been reconsidering you."

Elbert felt that he would burst if it took Coach any longer to get to the point.

"I've decided that perhaps we can make a place for a boy of your caliber on the team." Coach paused to wipe his forehead with a large green handkerchief.

"I'll try my best," Elbert burst forth, unable to contain himself any longer.

Coach smiled. "I know that you will; that's why I'm offering you the job."

Elbert stiffened slightly at the word "job." Coach must have made a mistake; surely he meant "position."

Coach placed his hand on Elbert's shoulder. "Will you be our team manager?" he asked.

For a moment everything in front of Elbert blurred. "Is that all that's available?" he managed to ask in a voice that was hardly more than a whisper.

"Afraid so, son." Coach's voice was gentle. "We'd like to have you join us," he added.

It was only one word, but it took Elbert an enormous effort to get it out. "Okay," he finally mumbled.

Mishmash

Elbert sat brooding on the locker-room bench, waiting for Dusty to get out of the shower so they could walk home together. As he sat, he turned the day's events over and over in his mind. Being manager would be fun, but it wasn't the same as having a position on the team. Well, he'd be manager for a while, he guessed. He'd have to. But not for one second longer than it took him to convince Coach to make him quarterback.

When Dusty appeared fully dressed, the boys took off.

Elbert was thoughtful. "Coach made me manager," he said at last.

Dusty clucked sympathetically.

Elbert looked at his shoes. "I guess it's better than nothing, but . . ."

Dusty nodded. "Too bad there isn't some way you could make the team."

"Sure, but how?" Elbert chewed on his lower lip. An idea was forming in his head. "Say, maybe I could use my tooth radio in some way. What do you think?"

"Thought reading you mean?"

"Yes."

"How would that help?"

Elbert hesitated. "I'm not sure. Maybe I could work out a way to impress Coach."

Dusty shook his head. "Sounds complicated. You can't do it just like that."

Elbert was secretly inclined to agree, but he wasn't about to give up that easily. "Well, maybe I can listen to what Coach is thinking and then surprise him by doing what he wants. That might work . . . somehow."

"Like what?"

Elbert considered for a moment. "Like if he's thinking of a certain play, I could come up with the answer even before he finished his question."

"Just like that?"

Elbert hedged. "Why not?"

"How do you know you can do it? You might get him awfully mad if you goofed. Maybe you'd better try this thought reading out first on someone else. Just to make sure that you can handle it okay."

"But why shouldn't it work? I've read my mother's and your mother's thoughts, and McGovern's and Coach's."

"If it were me I'd make sure that I was perfect at it before risking a thing like this. After all, if it backfires, Coach might throw you out altogether."

Elbert frowned. "I guess you're right," he admitted grudgingly. "Let's try it out when we get home."

Dusty shook his head slowly. "Can't," he said, "I'm stopping at Bracken's on the way home."

"How come? Your mother tell you to pick up some groceries?"

"Nope," Dusty answered. "I've been trying to get a job there, and old man Bracken told me to stop by today and he'd see if he could use me. If you want to stop with me, then maybe afterward I can help you."

Elbert decided that it might be helpful to have Dusty around when he tested his skill. "Okay, I'll wait for you," he answered.

Mr. Bracken stood behind the counter of his small and cluttered store, waiting on a tall, heavyset woman with a nose like a round red balloon.

She had a sour expression on her face — almost as sour as Mr. Bracken's.

Dusty nodded to the storekeeper and smiled his most friendly smile. Bracken gave him a brusque nod, while trying to keep up with the long list of items the woman had started to reel off. When he finally took a moment's pause, he jerked a finger at Dusty.

"Wait in the storeroom. I'm busy now," his high crackling voice announced sternly.

Dusty and Elbert turned on their heels, eager to duck into the back room. They made themselves comfortable sitting on some large cartons of canned goods. The room was even smaller than the front of the store, and the shelves were piled high with cans and other grocery items.

Elbert gazed at the crowded shelves. "He sure stocks enough for an army. He must have some business!"

Dusty smiled. "He's so busy that he forgets what he's doing and the place is a madhouse, my mother says. That's why I figured he could use some help in the store."

"What will you do?" Elbert asked. "Wait on customers?"

"Heck no, he'd never allow that," Dusty said. "But I could fill orders for him, or maybe help the man that he has doing deliveries."

"Hmmm," Elbert considered. "What you need to do is to impress him. Right?"

"Right," Dusty agreed.

Elbert grinned. "Suppose I help you get the job — how would that be?"

Dusty blinked. "How?" he demanded.

"By using my powers."

"How would you work it?"

Elbert grinned again. "I could tune in on him, find out what the order is, and you could fill it and have it all ready for him when he comes back here. That'll impress him."

Dusty ran his hand along the edge of the carton thoughtfully. "Do you think you can do it?"

"Why not?"

"Well, for one thing, Bracken's in the next room."

"I can try, can't I?"

"And besides, suppose he wonders how I knew what to do?" Dusty asked.

Elbert smiled. "Heck, he'll be so tickled that you've saved him time that he won't care how. He'll wonder how he ever got along without you."

"Yes, but won't it seem sort of weird?"

"We'll make him think he was so rushed that he gave you the order and forgot about it. You said yourself that he's forgetful."

Dusty had to agree. "Okay, try tuning him in," he finally answered.

Elbert drew the toothbrush out of his pocket and began the now familiar gyrations. Then he cocked his head so that he could listen more sharply.

"Hear anything yet?" Dusty whispered.

Elbert held his finger to his lips. It wasn't as easy as he had thought it would be. The static was pretty bad, and he seemed to be getting a number of conflicting waves. He adjusted his jaw and tilted his head in various directions, trying for clearer reception.

Dusty fidgeted, a questioning look in his eyes. Elbert moved uneasily on the carton. Maybe his powers wouldn't work under these conditions. Maybe he couldn't help Dusty after all. He was feeling pretty low when suddenly he heard a steady stream of thought.

"What's happening?" Dusty was asking impatiently, anxious to be in on what was going on.

Elbert fine-tuned as best he could. At last he began to hear the thoughts clearly. He held up his hand as if he were a traffic policeman. "Bracken's still taking down that woman's order. I'll tell you what I hear. Write it down," he hissed.

Dusty took out his pencil and grabbed a brown paper bag to write on.

". . . a jar of pickles — as sour as she is — two cans of tomatoes — as big and red as her nose — "

Dusty opened his mouth to speak, but Elbert's voice cut him off and he had to write quickly.

"One ginger . . ." The grocer's thoughts trailed off. Elbert cocked his head and worked his jaw frantically, but it was of no use. Ginger what? Elbert tried to decide quickly. Was it snaps, ale, or bread? To make sure, he called out all three items.

Dusty let out a long, low whistle and shook his writing hand in the air a few times to limber it up after he had finished.

Elbert motioned vigorously for Dusty to start writing again. ". . . eight chocolate puddings — gets any fatter and she'll bust," his voice rang out.

Dusty slapped his forehead with the flat of his palm.

Suddenly Elbert began to frown. Two sets of thoughts seemed to be coming in at the same time. He rattled his head and retuned. But there were still two thoughts booming in his head. He guessed that another customer had come into the shop. The messages came in so fast that Elbert couldn't take time to distinguish which was which without missing part of the reception. In order to keep up with all the waves, Elbert had to talk fast:

"A box of soap powder, bleach — bet she uses it on her hair. A tin of peanuts . . . beer and cigarettes with that." Elbert groaned. "Cross that out, the other customer said that."

Dusty looked at him as if he'd lost his mind.

". . . a container of bread crumbs," Elbert continued. "That Bracken's a crumb. If there were another grocery nearby . . . — What's that guy giving me the fish-eye for? I can't throw Mrs. Stouter out just to wait on him!"

Dusty put down the pencil. "Hey, come on, what's going on here?" he complained. "Just give me the order. Never mind the comments. I'm getting finger cramps!"

Elbert gave no indication of even having heard him. All his energy and attention were absorbed in trying to repeat the messages as they came through. ". . . two packages of macaroni — she's too fat for that, take it out."

Dusty had given up writing and was grabbing the items off the open shelves and piling them on the floor. "Well, is it in or out?" he asked wearily. He had given up understanding what was going on.

"One can of clams, two jars of herring," Elbert went on without stopping. He kept calling out items one after another. Finally he came to a stop. The boys looked in dismay at the pile of groceries on the floor.

"We'd better find a large carton and start packing all this," Elbert directed, sliding down from his perch. "Mrs. Stouter wants it delivered this after-

60

noon. Bracken has a man waiting to give him another order, and he's worried about getting Mrs. Stouter's stuff out in time."

The boys worked feverishly stuffing the items on the floor into a carton. When they were done, it was filled to overflowing. They sat down exhausted, to wait for the storekeeper. Before they could see him they could hear the old man muttering.

"Too much to do . . . selling, filling, getting orders out on time . . . impatient customers . . . too much . . . too much!"

Elbert elbowed Dusty. "Wait till he sees what you've done! Boy, will he be happy."

The boys didn't have long to wait. Mr. Bracken, who was busily looking at the slips of paper that he held in his hand, stumbled across the huge packed carton which stood directly in his path in the center aisle of the room. His steel-rimmed glasses slid to the tip of his nose and his papers went flying. "What's that?" he demanded, pointing to the carton. Without waiting for an answer, he continued. "Been playing store, eh? I've enough to do around here without any make-believe. People to wait on . . . orders to take . . . orders to fill . . . it's more than man can stand!"

Dusty took a step forward. "That's why we filled Mrs. Stouter's order for you . . . to help out."

The storekeeper frowned and poked among the

bulging items. "She never bought that much," he complained. "Beer . . . she doesn't drink." He flung the carton of cigarettes aside. "She doesn't smoke," he roared. The old man turned and faced the boys. "Anyway, I never gave you her order!" he cried accusingly. "What do you kids think you're doing — reading my mind? Look at that load!" The storekeeper flung his arms wide. "All needs to be put back. Double work!"

Elbert looked guiltily at Dusty. He had evidently included what the other customer had been thinking. And now he'd made a mishmash of the whole order.

Mr. Bracken rocked on his heels and then went on. "Thought I might try a helper, but now I see that it's useless. Just makes more work for me, and I've enough as it is."

"But I . . ." Dusty tried to explain.

"Get out, while I still have the strength to talk. GO!" Mr. Bracken cut Dusty's attempted explanation short, pointing his finger at the back door.

The boys looked at each other in desperation.

"Go on!"

Elbert grabbed Dusty's arm and they moved to the door. As soon as they were outside, Dusty pulled his arm free.

"You sure fixed that one for me," he groaned.

Elbert swallowed hard. "I thought it would help. I really did."

Dusty threw him a withering look. "You thought . . . he thought . . . the other guy thought . . . Mrs. Stouter thought . . . Maybe it would be better for everyone to keep their thoughts to themselves. It might cause less trouble!"

Elbert kept pace in silence. It was true: reading people's minds didn't always work out the way you expected. The big question was, would it work on Coach?

Girl Trouble

Mr. Berry made a big deal over Elbert's joining the team as manager. He retold many stories of his own school team, and he advised Elbert about all the things the manager had done to boost morale and to make the team the winner it was.

Elbert was pleased that his father seemed happy with his new job, but somehow he couldn't get as all fired up about it as his father. He had a gnawing feeling that his dad was trying to make him feel good. The more Mr. Berry pep-talked him, the more Elbert became determined to make a position on the team. Then everything would really be as rosy as Mr. Berry was painting it.

There was a way, but Elbert wrestled with the problem. Should he or should he not read Coach's mind? Would it work . . . or . . . ? Elbert's feelings wavered back and forth. When he was by himself he listened to his radio. It was especially comforting at night, lulling him off to sleep, and letting him escape from thoughts about how best to use his powers to influence Coach.

He had dug up his old portable camp toothbrush that folded back on a hinge to make it very tiny. But as yet he had not taken it to school. He convinced himself that he was surveying the situation — the sensible thing to do before taking action. He didn't want to take any chances and perhaps forfeit his place with the team if Coach should become angry.

Being manager allowed Elbert to share in almost everything that the team did, but that still wasn't good enough. He made it a point to become friendly with Scott, who had the distinction of being Rivertown High's first-team quarterback. Although he never let any of the fellows see him at it, when he was alone at home, Elbert practiced everything that Scott was learning, Most of the strategy he already knew because of his father's teaching, but he practiced anyway so that he could learn Coach's way of doing things.

He still hesitated about using his special powers. First he wanted to make sure of his ground. No sense in messing things up as he had done for Dusty.

66

Elbert rather enjoyed Scott's company, especially since Dusty was still acting rather cool toward him. Scott was fun to be with, except that he acted funny about one of their classmates named Merry. Whenever she was around, Elbert noticed that Scott paid a lot of attention to her. Of course she was pretty, but that was no reason to spend so much time with a girl, Elbert thought, or to think about her on the field.

These past few days Scott didn't seem to have his mind on football at all. He was fumbling in handing off to the halfback, and Elbert had already given up counting the number of times that he hadn't received from center properly. Coach had bawled Scott out a few times and kept him after scrimmage to practice.

Elbert ached to substitute. His hands itched to feel the ball, and his leg muscles got so tight that they felt as if they'd pop. But Coach never looked his way.

The whole team had taken to walking around with long faces these days. The Sampson game was not far off, and it didn't even look as if the team would make it through this week's game with Jackson High, which was usually considered a pushover. Elbert was even gloomier than the teammates. So far he hadn't dared to attempt his scheme to impress Coach, and now the team's good name was in jeopardy. Elbert knew that the time to act had come.

At the next practice session Elbert was among the first on the field. His mind raced with ideas, and he patted his shirt pocket confidently. The portable toothbrush hardly made a bulge. At first all the boys scrambled out on the field, did a few isometric exercises, then split up into two teams for scrimmage.

Elbert sat down on the bench next to the three extra players while Coach paced on the sidelines, shouting instructions to the two teams. As they lined up, Elbert could see that once again Scott was acting peculiarly. First he forgot to put in his mouth guard, then he held up the game because he had forgotten to lace his shoes. At this rate he'd never remember the plays, and from the look on Coach's face there was going to be trouble.

Without attracting too much attention, Elbert slipped off the bench and squatted down behind it with his back to the field. He whipped out the toothbrush, snapped the hinge, and began to brush. He hadn't gone over the filling more than twice when he felt a steady breeze of hot breath down his neck. Turning slightly, he found a curious face poking over his shoulder. It was Rick, one of the team's ends.

"Whatcha doing that for?" he inquired.

Elbert felt his face growing hot, and his hand fell from his mouth.

68

"You crazy-clean or something?" Rick asked. He poked Jim who was sitting next to him. "Get a load of Mr. Clean," he cracked.

Elbert tried being as nonchalant as he could. "I've got something stuck in my tooth," he mumbled. "I sure do," he thought to himself.

"You always carry a toothbrush with you?" Jim asked.

"Always wants to be prepared — a regular Boy Scout!" Rick slapped his thigh and laughed.

Elbert ground his teeth together and tried to stare the boys down, but static roared so loud in his head that he bared his teeth and his eyes became narrow slits.

"Hey, what's that noise?" Jim leaned forward to listen more carefully.

Rick cocked his head to hear better. "Sounds like radio static to me," he answered. He got up off the bench and approached Elbert. "Come on now, boy, don't tell me you carry a radio too!" He laughed as if he had told a joke.

Elbert quickly closed his mouth and spread his jaws as widely as he could so that his teeth could not possibly touch. He knew that he must look peculiar with his chin stretched so low, but he tried to act as if he didn't have any idea of what Rick meant.

Rick threw back his head and laughed louder. "Maybe he swallowed a radio!" he suggested.

"Anyone who walks around brushing his teeth when he doesn't have to would do anything," Jim declared.

Elbert stood quietly and braced himself for the next jibe, but it never came. A sudden roar from the field caught the boys' attention immediately. Scott had fumbled again, and Coach was bellowing louder than ever.

Elbert sat down heavily. Even though his secret had almost been discovered, he couldn't abandon his plan. The rumpus on the field died down and the game continued. Jim and Rick had evidently forgotten about him, because they were intent on the game again. Gingerly Elbert closed his jaws. He listened carefully, but the signal coming in was so faint that he couldn't make head or tail out of it.

This time Elbert was very careful to move away from the bench and turn so that no one could see him before he brought out the brush again. He attacked the tooth vigorously and quickly, stuffing the toothbrush back into his pocket the moment he was through. The bench warmers were all intent on the plays, and Elbert was able to move nearer without attracting their attention. Coach stood nearby.

Elbert devoted all his powers of concentration to tuning in Coach. It was hard, because the thoughts of the boys on the bench and from the nearby field made for strong interference. At last Elbert stopped fighting it and began to listen.

"If Coach keeps me after scrimmage today, Merry will hit the roof. Bet she'll go out with that Baker guy from tenth grade instead of me." Elbert recognized the thinker at once. It was Scott; his thoughts had been so overpowering that Elbert could not get through to Coach. "But golly, I can't help it if I'm stuck with football practice instead of being able to take Merry for a soda after school. Wish I knew how to get her all for myself."

A sudden shout made Elbert hold his ears. He looked up to find Coach yelling at Scott at the top of his lungs.

"What the deuce are you thinking about, Scott? You should have been over there." Coach ran out onto the field. He was pointing vigorously to a spot, as if he could move Scott there with the gesture alone.

Elbert could see Scott slump dejectedly, and his thoughts came through slow and clear, "Gosh, here I go again. Merry will clobber me if I'm late today."

Coach was red-faced and fuming. "If you can't keep your mind on the game, Scott, we might as well hand the win to Jackson. And as far as Sampson goes — they'll probably slaughter us!"

Everyone groaned, and all eyes turned to stare at Scott, who was busy making a circle in the dirt with the toe of his shoe. Elbert felt a wave of sympathy for him. No one knew how awful Scott felt or why.

Elbert guessed that this would be the perfect time to impress Coach. Then Coach might even decide to let him play in Saturday's game, if he were hard-pressed enough. And yet Elbert had grown very fond of Scott. He knew how proud he was of his position.

Much as he wanted to be quarterback, Elbert had a nagging feeling that he should help Scott rather than take advantage of him and attempt to steal his position. It wasn't an easy decision. What should he do?

Elbert to the Rescue

AFTER SHOWERS, the boys began to leave for home. Elbert sat in the locker room waiting for Scott. He was sure now that he wanted to help him. But how? Elbert was lost in thought when a familiar voice hailed him.

"Going home now? I'll walk you."

Elbert looked up to find Dusty standing over him. Without a second thought Elbert jumped up from the bench. It was the first time in days that Dusty had acted downright friendly. Elbert was about to join him when he suddenly remembered about Scott, and he hesitated.

"You coming?" Dusty demanded.

"I, uh . . . I thought I'd wait for Scott," Elbert explained lamely.

"After the way he's been fouling things up lately he needs a friend," Dusty muttered.

"He really can't help it." Elbert hadn't meant to tell, but it just slipped out.

"Oh, he can't, eh? Well he'd better, and in a hurry too, or we'll lose the darn game Saturday," Dusty answered bitterly.

"That's why I was waiting for him. I thought I'd help him."

"You? What can you do?"

Elbert beckoned Dusty into a corner. "Scott's been having trouble with Merry. Baker's muscling in and Scott wants her all for himself. He's worried. His mind's on that instead of the game."

"How'd you know?"

Elbert pointed to his mouth.

Dusty whistled. "So what can you do?" he asked.

"I thought maybe I could find a way to fix things between them by reading her mind," Elbert declared.

Dusty stroked his chin pensively. "Let me get this straight. You figure if you find out how Scott can get her just for himself, he'll keep his mind on the game and we can win?"

Elbert stuck out his lower lip and nodded.

"But you can't tell him about *this*." Dusty pointed to Elbert's jaw.

Elbert frowned. "Guess not," he agreed.

"Maybe you could read Merry's mind and sort of let it slip about what he should do. It'd be worth a try. Do you think you can do it alone?"

Elbert's eyebrows drew together in a worried frown. "Maybe if you'd help out too, we could swing it," he answered.

Dusty nodded in agreement. "Okay. We gotta stand together and pull the team through."

Elbert felt better than he had in days. Dusty was acting like his old self again.

They didn't have long to wait before Scott emerged from the shower with a face as woebegone as a bloodhound's. He was the last one out, having been detained by Coach for a lecture. All the other boys had long since gone.

When Elbert and Dusty settled on the bench next to Scott's locker, he threw them an anxious glance. As he dressed he didn't say much. It was as though he couldn't decide whether they were angry, like the rest of the team, or just being friendly.

"Too bad Coach let you have it," Elbert sympathized.

Scott's face relaxed. "Honest, guys, I didn't mean to foul up the plays," he said dejectedly.

Elbert and Dusty nodded understandingly.

"Going home now?" Elbert asked him.

"Nope. Planned to hop over to the Sweet Shop."

"We'll join you," Dusty put in quickly.

76

Scott ran his tongue over his lips. "I'm meeting someone," he said in a low voice.

The boys ignored this and fell in step as he took off.

"What's the rush, Scott?" Dusty asked.

"Uh . . . I told you — I gotta meet someone."

"Who?" Dusty insisted.

"For Pete's sake, you're nosy," Scott exploded. "It's Merry, that's who."

Elbert gave Dusty the high sign. "Why rush for a girl? She wouldn't rush for you."

"Yeah, you're right," Scott muttered, but he didn't slow down.

"You don't need her anyway. Girls interfere. They're a waste of time," Dusty advised.

Scott snickered and quickened his pace, and Elbert hurried along to keep up with him.

"Girls and football don't mix," he warned, but it seemed to make no impression on Scott.

They continued in silence, Scott hustling them through the streets until they arrived at the Sweet Shop.

As they entered the shop, Dusty nudged Elbert in the ribs. "There she is at the counter," he whispered.

Merry was staring angrily at the large clock which hung over the counter. Scott took the empty seat next to her, and Dusty and Elbert sat on the next two stools along the counter. Merry eyed the three of them in silence.

"Got stuck at practice," Scott began sheepishly. Merry sniffed.

Elbert leaned forward and looked at her. He liked the way her long dark hair cascaded loosely down her back. Yes, Merry was a pretty girl, and being angry gave her an impish air which Elbert had to admit was attractive.

"We're all working hard because of the game on Saturday," Dusty was saying.

"We can't let anything interfere," Elbert interrupted. "Scott's a great quarterback, and he's very important to the team."

"Is he?" Merry's voice was as sweet as honey.

"Positively," Dusty put in.

The clerk came and took their orders, and Elbert walked over to the jukebox as casually as he could. He had to use his toothbrush. He leaned down, pretending to examine the selections, and quickly agitated his filling. Concentrating on Merry, he made his way back to the counter. He hoped she would be thinking about Scott, so that he could find out what to tell him. He took a sip of his soda and then clamped his teeth shut to listen.

"Why didn't I ever notice *him* before? He's kinda cute. Oh, those freckles!" It was Merry coming in clearly.

Elbert searched Scott's face and then Dusty's;

neither had a sign of a freckle. He thought about Baker. Baker didn't have freckles either.

". . . wonder if he'd be fun to date? I bet he'd be on time." Merry's thoughts tuned in perfectly.

Elbert caught her eye.

"I'll bet *you* wouldn't keep me waiting," she cooed at him.

Elbert blinked and Dusty's eyebrows rose. Scott moved uneasily on his seat.

"Scott's going to win the game for us," Elbert gulped. "Just wait till you see him go."

"Is he?" Merry purred. "Isn't he cute . . . he's blushing!" she was thinking.

Elbert could feel the red creeping up the back of his neck. He looked away, but not fast enough to miss the big broad wink that Merry threw him.

"Come on, think about Scott," Elbert pleaded silently. He wished that he could think of a way to direct her thoughts. Elbert breathed easier when Merry turned to Scott and began to talk quietly to him. He felt a nudge and realized that Dusty was after his attention.

"Hear anything?" Dusty asked.

"Nothing worth repeating," Elbert muttered.

"What'll we tell him? Better think up something."

Elbert knew he couldn't tell Scott what he had heard. He made one more attempt at listening. Merry was already thinking of leaving. It seemed that she wanted to stop at the library, and she was

80

wondering whether to take out a love story or a mystery. Elbert gave up. It amazed him how a girl could talk to a fellow about one thing and be thinking about another. Elbert wondered why Scott wanted to get involved with a girl in the first place!

"Bye, Elbert." It was Merry taking her leave. Elbert nodded, as did Dusty, but Scott was looking after her with a lingering look.

"Will I see you tomorrow?" Scott asked anxiously.

"Maybe," Merry answered with a giggle, and started toward the door.

"Scott looks like a sick cow," Elbert thought. "What a nut!" But it wasn't up to him to decide whether Scott should like her. It was only up to him to advise on a plan of action.

No sooner had she gone that Scott turned toward Elbert. "Lay off her," he snapped.

"Wouldn't think of muscling in," Elbert answered. — "Scott sure is a jealous type when it comes to girls," he thought. "First he's worried about Baker, and now he thinks I'm interested in Merry."

But for the team's sake Elbert had to think up some way to put Scott's mind at ease. He had to find a way to get Merry to show that she preferred Scott to anyone else. A glimmer of an idea began to form in his head and Elbert smiled to himself.

"Want me to tell you how to operate?" he asked Scott. "I know just what you have to do to make Merry like you best of all!"

Defeat

ELBERT TOOK ONE ARM and Dusty the other, and between them they hustled Scott out of the Sweet Shop. Once on the sidewalk Scott freed himself and confronted Elbert.

"How?" he pleaded. "How can I make Merry like me the best?"

Elbert folded his arms across his chest, and his voice lowered an octave. "Merry likes you well enough, but she likes others too."

Scott groaned.

"If you want her to like you best of all, then you'll have to become a hero."

"What do you mean . . . like rescue someone?"

Elbert shook his head. Sometimes Scott was

thick. "A football hero. If you're a hero and win the game on Saturday, you'll be tops with her."

"Are you sure?"

"Of course. Girls love football heroes. You'll be in, and guys like Baker and me will be out."

Scott's eyes lit up and he swayed slightly. "I'll be in, Baker out," he crooned softly.

Elbert nodded and Dusty beamed. Scott stood blinking before them. And then he slowly began to wag his head.

"Look," he began miserably, "how can I be a hero when I'm forever fouling things up?"

Elbert spoke firmly. "That's easy. You can play okay when you keep your mind on it."

Scott nodded absentmindedly.

"So we'll keep reminding you to play well, so that the team will win the game and you'll be a hero and win Merry," Elbert finished triumphantly.

Scott looked slowly from Elbert to Dusty and back again. Then he scratched his chin and glanced up at the sky. He showed no inclination to hurry a decision. Finally his mouth opened. "Me in, Baker out," he breathed.

Elbert and Dusty exchanged quick glances. "Right!" they chimed together.

Scott spit on the ground. "Okay, guys. Keep after me. Don't let me rest a minute." His voice had suddenly taken on new determinaton.

"It's a deal," Elbert and Dusty agreed, and all of them shook hands on it.

Elbert and Dusty were true to their bargain. They didn't let Scott moon around for a second. Elbert invented some cheers to keep him on his toes.

When Scott was ready to walk out on the practice field, Elbert would come up behind him and whisper:

If you win,
You'll be in!

And during a game Dusty would sidle up to Scott and mutter:

You'll score a zero,
If you're no hero!

Scott had little time to let his mind wander. By Saturday he was performing at his top level. The team's morale was at a new high, and Elbert, Dusty, and Scott rejoiced.

The sun shone brightly on Saturday. The sky was blue, with occasional lazy clouds drifting across it in patches. The Rivertown High team sprinted out on the field confidently. Jackson was as good as dead already. Dusty jogged alongside Scott, who grinned broadly at Elbert, sitting on the sidelines.

When his friends were directly in front of him, Elbert whispered out of the corner of his mouth:

> Win the game,
> You've got the dame!

Scott held up his thumb and forefinger in the shape of an O. Elbert settled back with a sigh. At least if he couldn't be quarterback he had helped his team to win by getting Scott back into shape.

The Jackson boys looked pretty massive as they maneuvered on the field. Elbert glanced over at his own team. They seemed to be functioning smoothly. Scott apparently had his mind on the business at hand, even though he hadn't done anything very spectacular yet. He had held the ball a few times and had made some yardage, but the Jackson tackles had been on his heels and brought him down before any score could be made.

Elbert watched Scott untangle himself from the heap in the middle of the field as the two teams piled up in a deadlock. And then at last it seemed as if Scott was to get his chance. He had the ball.

Elbert rose from the bench. "Scott . . . Scott . . . give 'em all you've got!" he roared.

Scott seemed to be responding to the cheer. He began the long trek toward the goal line. Thunder-

ing down the field, he threaded his way through the opposing tackles. On he ran, dodging and turning past his opponents. Elbert shouted until his throat felt as if it would crack from dryness. The Jackson boys lunged at Scott, grabbing at his legs, thrusting at his shoulders, but it seemed as if nothing could stop him.

Elbert couldn't resist. With everyone so absorbed, surely no one would notice. He was dying to know what Scott was thinking. He whipped out his toothbrush, snapped the hinge, and in one slick, practiced gesture agitated his filling. The waves started almost immediately. Of course they were confused, but after a few moments Elbert was lucky enough to tune in to Scott.

"If I win, then I'm in!" Scott was coming in weakly, but clearly enough to be understood.

Elbert grinned; he had done a good job with Scott. But his smile did not last for very long. Scott's thoughts were changing, and that might spell trouble. Elbert held his ears to shut out all the other surrounding noises, and concentrated hard.

"Got to do something great — something that will really knock her off her feet — be a hero!"

Elbert rose to his feet and waved his arms frantically. "Just score — don't show off, Scott!" he yelled.

But already he was too late, even if Scott could

have heard him. Scott was making his way into a collision course with Jackson's toughest tackle. It was plain to Elbert that Scott had not seen him at first, and that when he did he decided to shoulder right past the Jackson boy by using some fancy footwork. But just as he approached him the tackle shifted his position and by crouching low caught Scott in the gut with his powerful right shoulder. Within seconds the other players had overtaken them and piled on in a huge pyramid.

As they peeled off they exposed Scott, who lay still on the bottom of the heap. Elbert stood up wearily. Victory had been so close, and now . . . He lifted his hands and shrugged, and his glance fell on the toothbrush still clutched in his hand. "A lot of good *that* did," he muttered in disgust, and turned to find Jim staring at him.

"For your information, the game isn't played with a toothbrush, Mr. Clean," Jim grunted. "It's a ball you're supposed to carry!"

Elbert jammed the brush into his pocket and was trying not to betray his irritation when he noticed Coach, the team's doctor, and a number of other people running out onto the field. Within minutes a stretcher was being brought, and Elbert could see that Scott was being lifted onto it. Elbert broke into a run toward the crowd, arriving just in time to help escort Scott off the field. Scott had a sheepish look on his face as he gazed up at Elbert.

"Guess I fouled that up," he murmured. Elbert was about to agree when he was elbowed aside by a sharp thrust. He looked around to find Merry fighting her way to Scott's side.

"Scott . . . Scott . . . are you all right?" she kept murmuring.

Elbert's eyes popped. There was no figuring women. He thought surely that she'd be through with Scott after his performance today, and yet here she was fussing over him.

"The doctor says it's not a bad break," Scott was reassuring her, "just my ankle." His face was red as a sunset, but he was all smiles.

Yea, Scott! Yea, Scott!
The best we've got.
Good try . . . good try . . . good try!

It was the crowd in the grandstand cheering loudly.

Elbert looked over at Scott. He didn't even seem to hear the cheers; he was completely absorbed in what Merry was saying. Elbert strained his ears to catch it.

"You're a real hero," she was cooing.

Elbert caught Scott's eye for a second, and the fallen hero blushed. Elbert watched as Scott was carried off to the locker room, with Merry hovering close by his side.

"There goes the game," he heard someone mutter. He looked around and saw that Coach was giving last-minute instructions to Steve, who was going in as quarterback. Elbert groaned. Steve was a tall, sturdy boy whose size had gotten him on the team. He meant well, but he wasn't much on figuring out plays.

The next few minutes went just as Elbert feared: Jackson scored and Rivertown went down in defeat. The game was lost — not only this game, but probably the one next week with Sampson as well. The whole team knew it. Elbert clenched his fists.

Hope for Elbert

THE TEAM WAS ALREADY ON THE PRACTICE FIELD doing their exercises when Elbert got there on Monday afternoon. Instead of sitting down on the bench to watch, as he usually did, he joined the group. Somehow, someway, he was determined to show Coach what he could do on the field. Coach lifted his eyebrows, but apparently didn't feel it was worth his time to question Elbert's actions.

When the boys split up into groups for individual drill practice, Elbert considered which one he would join. Some of the boys were practicing kicking, others passing and catching, and still others were tackling dummies. Elbert waited to see where Coach was going to observe. He hoped it wouldn't be the tackling group. Tackling was not exactly his strong point. Elbert's eyes brightened. Coach was making his way over to the boys who were kicking, and Elbert sprinted to join that group.

Elbert thought Coach looked a little melancholy as he watched the boys. Without seeming consciously to be doing it, Elbert lined up for a turn. One after another the boys came up to kick, and Coach analyzed and criticized each one in turn. Some kicks were off balance, others too short. The boys were so occupied with trying to do their best under Coach's watchful gaze that no one seemed to notice that Elbert had come up for a turn.

Elbert poised for the kick. The ball snapped back; out shot his right foot. The moment it connected he knew that it would be a good one. All the lessons that his father had given him, plus all the practicing that he had done in the summer, had combined to educate his toe. The low whistles of the boys acknowledged it.

"Now, *that's* a kick!" Coach voiced his approval loudly and turned to praise the player. When he spotted Elbert his smile clouded. "Who made that kick?" he asked, addressing himself to the group in general.

Elbert took a step forward.

Coach blinked and pushed back his cap. He eyed Elbert with interest for a moment, and then shrugged. "Lucky kick, son," he declared, "real lucky."

Elbert stood before him expectantly. It was obvious that Coach was impressed, yet he was not reacting the way Elbert had hoped he would. Before he could call further attention to himself Coach was again speaking to the group.

"Keep up the practice. Remember the pointers that I gave you." Then Coach turned on his heel and moved toward another group.

As soon as he had gone, the boys relaxed.

"That was a swell kick, Elbert," Bob admitted.

"Sure was," the others chorused.

"Bet we could use you," Rick put in.

Without answering, Elbert strode off. He could hear the boys muttering after him.

"What's eating him? Hand him a compliment and he acts like he didn't hear."

Elbert squared his shoulders. He didn't have time to explain things to them. He shaded his eyes and looked across the field. Coach was just approaching the boys who were practicing passing and catching. Elbert speeded up. This time he stood slightly on the sidelines, waiting for a chance to enter the play. He watched closely. Dusty had the ball and was throwing a long pass. From the way they were set up, Elbert could see at a glance that Jim was supposed to receive. Elbert kept his eye on Jim. He wasn't moving quite fast enough to get under the ball. Elbert calculated the ball's path quickly. It was headed straight toward him. All he need do was step onto the field and receive it.

Without a second thought, his feet moved. He raised his arms, and the ball entered them as if it were a homing pigeon. He spun on his heel and galloped down the field at top speed. Elbert could hear shouting behind him, but he didn't stop until he'd gone enough distance to impress Coach. Then he turned and trotted back to the group.

"Hey, whatcha think you're doing?" the boys greeted him.

Elbert sought Coach's face. Coach stood straight and tall, his hands on his hips. Elbert looked for the welcoming smile, but it wasn't there. Instead of approval, Coach's eyebrows were drawn into one low, dark line across his eyes. His mouth was puckered in a frown. When Elbert came abreast of him he spoke.

"Doesn't it occur to you, young man, that we're having enough trouble whipping this team into shape before Saturday without having the manager run off with the ball?" he said testily.

Elbert's shoulders sagged. Coach hadn't paid the slightest attention to his playing ability. The only thing he had concluded was that Elbert was making a pest of himself. Elbert handed over the ball, looked down at his feet, and mumbled, "I'm sorry."

Coach acknowledged his apology brusquely. "All right, boys, now that you've got the ball again, try to hang on to it," Coach said gruffly. "As for you," he added, directing his words toward Elbert, "let the players do the playing." With that he strode off.

Elbert kicked at the dirt.

"That was a great play," Dusty whispered to him as he passed. "You really belong on the team."

Elbert put his hands in his pockets and trudged back to the sidelines. He only wished that what Dusty had said was true. But here was Monday shot and no progress made, and there wasn't much more time until the Sampson game.

It was pouring when Elbert got up the next morning. As he dressed he worked his teeth, tuning in his radio. The news was about over, and the weatherman was predicting a 70 per cent chance of showers all day. Elbert wiggled his head, hoping in some way to change the prediction. His father was always saying that the weatherman would know more if he'd look out the window.

Mr. Berry didn't have much faith in weather predictions. He claimed that if the announcer said that there was a 70 per cent chance of rain, that meant seven of the ten guys at the station thought it would rain! Elbert hoped his father was right. Meanwhile he went downstairs and ate his breakfast. Before leaving the house, he tucked his toothbrush in his pocket.

But despite Elbert's hopes, the rain fell solidly all day. At school dismissal Elbert ran for the locker room with Dusty.

"Rotten break . . . this rain," Dusty mumbled. "We could sure use the time on the field."

Elbert couldn't have agreed more. Now he would be wasting another precious day. He bit off a fingernail and worked it through his teeth to console himself.

The boys settled themselves on the benches in the locker room, and Coach briefed them once again on offensive formations and defensive alignments. He particularly dwelt on the umbrella 4-3. Elbert had to admit that Coach had picked a formation with a perfect name for a rainy day. Elbert had memorized the wing right and wing left offensive formations long ago, and he studied the single wing and short punt with renewed interest. No sense in wasting the day entirely, he decided, as he committed them to memory. He didn't bother with the toothbrush. He had no chance to go off by himself to use it, and he wasn't about to risk having the entire team catching him at it.

When the team assembled on the field the next

day, the sun shone brilliantly. Elbert was in high spirits. Time was getting short, and he had decided to risk using his special powers. He was the last to leave the locker room. Before he walked out he gave his filling a good workout. As he moved past the lineup, he began receiving waves.

"Hope we get through early. I got a load of homework to do . . . Wonder why we're bothering? Sampson will slaughter us . . . My shoes must be getting small . . . My dad will kill me if I don't get the car cleaned today . . ."

Elbert was about to sit down on the sidelines when someone on the bench hailed him.

"Come on over here." It was Scott with his foot all done up in a cast.

Elbert waved and trotted over.

"It doesn't feel so bad," Scott answered Elbert's question. "Except I feel rotten when I think about Saturday."

Elbert asked about Merry and Scott assured him that the plan had worked out fine. "I owe you a lot, pal," he admitted.

Scott turned to watch the team work out, while Elbert settled back to work his jaw. After a while he was able to fine-tune Coach in:

"If I could only drill good judgment into Steve, he wouldn't be so bad," Coach was thinking. "But, then he's not too fast on his feet either . . . oh well

97

. . . dum, dum, tee, dum . . . dum, tee, dum, dum, dum, tee, dum."

Elbert recognized the funeral march, and he closed his eyes. He was interrupted again by Coach's thoughts:

"It's going to be heck for morale if we get clobbered. If we only had a decent quarterback, we could make it!"

Now Coach was approaching the bench. He sat down between Elbert and Scott, while continuing to shout orders to the boys on the field. Elbert leaned closer and the reception blared in his head. Quickly he tuned it down and listened.

"Now what's Steve going to call for this one?" Coach was thinking.

Elbert watched intently. He could see at a glance that the boys were falling into the wrong positions.

Coach stood up. "No, no, NO!" he bellowed. "The umbrella. I just drilled you in it yesterday!"

Elbert's head felt as if it had been hit with a bomb as Coach's thoughts and voice exploded so closely, and at the same time.

"All right, all right. Now try this." Coach set the teams up in another play. Then he sank down heavily on the bench. "If only we had a clear head out there," Elbert could hear him thinking. His own head felt far from clear after that last burst of sound.

Elbert watched the boys maneuver. "Calls for a

strong right formation," he muttered, even before he could hear Coach's thoughts on the matter.

Coach turned abruptly. "You're right!" he shouted.

Elbert looked over his shoulder quickly. He couldn't believe that Coach was talking to him.

Coach scratched his head and squinted his eyes into narrow slits. "You can run pretty fast, can't you?"

Elbert nodded.

"You can kick too, eh?"

Elbert grinned broadly. At last things were going as he had planned.

"It seems that you can think too." Coach smiled.

Elbert could feel the back of his neck getting warm.

Coach's eyes slid over Elbert's undersized frame and the smile disappeared from his face.

Elbert could hear Coach thinking: "It'd be slaughter if they ever brought him down." Elbert wanted to shout that he was sure that he would be okay, but his mouth seemed frozen shut.

Finally Coach put his hand on Elbert's shoulder. "Elbert, I'd like to use you, I really would, but I . . ."

Elbert's heart sank at what he knew was coming.

"Tell you what, son, I've got to use Steve . . ."

Elbert braced himself. He guessed that he was

about to be offered another *job* with the team as a consolation.

". . . but since Scott is out and only Steve is available . . ."

Elbert held his breath.

". . . we will need a sub . . . just in case."

Elbert couldn't believe his ears. It wasn't a promise that he could play, but it was a *position* on the team. He threw back his shoulders and raised his head. He was on his way!

Triumph at Last

IF MR. BERRY WAS HAPPY when Elbert had told him about being named team manager, he was ecstatic when he learned that his son had become a sub. This time Elbert wholeheartedly joined in the reaction. It was as if the entire world had really taken on a rosy glow.

At the dinner table each night Mr. Berry talked so much about football that Elbert could see his mother beginning to get annoyed. But though he felt sorry for her, having to sit through his father's old football glories, plus having to hear about the Rivertown team, he enjoyed the man-to-man talk. His mother was really a good sport about the whole thing, and Elbert knew that she was happy for him.

She took particular pains in adjusting the uniform that he was given so that it fitted properly, and she was duly impressed by his new helmet.

When it rained for the next two days, Mr. and Mrs. Berry were as gloomy as Elbert. But the team practiced in the gym. Elbert joined in running exercises, push-ups, rope climbing, skull sessions, and isometrics, but he avoided tackling the dummies. He knew that if Coach ever saw him at that he might change his mind about the whole deal.

Coach wasn't too strict about Elbert's training, although he made sure that he was fitted for a mouth guard. Elbert got the feeling that Coach didn't really think that he would get into the game unless the circumstances were quite unusual.

Some of the boys hoped that the game would be rained out on Saturday, but the day was ushered in by warm fall sunshine. Elbert could hardly wait for game time. He and Dusty left early for the football field and talked for a while in the locker room as they made last-minute adjustments in their uniforms. Elbert's mouth guard was delivered just in time for him to take it along with his other gear when he left the locker room.

As the team trotted out on the field, Elbert took a seat next to Scott and the other boys who were bench warmers. He squinted up at the stands and spotted his folks. His father was standing and gesturing, obviously explaining something to his mother. Suddenly they saw him and waved. Elbert nodded and then turned back to the field.

The Sampson team came sprinting out. They looked a great deal larger than the other teams that Rivertown High had played. Coach was giving Steve some last-minute advice, and then he joined the boys on the bench. Elbert could see that he looked worried.

The action started, and Coach sat muttering advice that the team couldn't possibly hear. The two teams seemed to pile up in deadlock after deadlock. Although Rivertown was not making any score, the linesmen were playing an excellent defensive game. Then the Sampson quarterback got through and the score was 6 to 0.

The Sampson rooters shouted and stamped, their noisemakers resounding in the air. They kicked for the extra point but failed; the Rivertown team blocked it beautifully. As the game continued, Rivertown didn't score, but at least they kept Sampson from getting any more points. The score still stood 6 to 0 at the end of the half.

During the second half Steve took the ball a number of times, but because he lacked speed and couldn't decide on the correct tactics, he was always brought down before he got very far. Elbert sat on the bench chewing on his fingernails. He kept hoping that Coach would put him in, but Coach never seemed to look at him. The third quarter passed and Elbert began to wonder if he'd ever get into the game. Elbert heard Coach muttering to himself. He leaned closer to catch what he was saying:

". . . great defensive. Those linesmen are remembering everything that I taught them. Wish we could tie the score. If only Steve would call the right plays, or guess what Sampson has in mind and intercept." Coach moved restlessly on the bench. "Oh well, Steve's trying his best — he's no mind reader, and that's what we need!"

Elbert could hardly restrain himself from blurting out, "He's not, but *I* am!"

Coach had gotten up from the bench and was walking up and down the sidelines, following the plays and giving instructions whenever possible. Elbert knew that he had to find a private spot. The only thing that might get him into the game was his toothbrush. He had to use it!

He edged off the seat and squatted down behind Scott. "He won't give me away if he notices," Elbert felt sure. He whipped out the brush, shoved it into his mouth, and gave the filling a workout. Then he eased himself back onto the bench. Everyone was so intent on the game that no one had noticed his actions.

The air rang with a cheer from the Sampson

cheerleaders. Elbert moved uneasily in his seat. He had to maneuver a lot before he was able to tune in on Sampson's quarterback. It wasn't easy to eliminate all the other voices that came to him. But at last he was sure that he had connected with his man, and was able to sit back and listen.

". . . team's a pushover if we could only knock out these linesmen again. What a break for us that Scott can't play. That guy they have in is strictly second string," Elbert heard the quarterback thinking.

Elbert found himself making a fist. He clenched his teeth and listened harder.

". . . that guy picks the simplest plays. It's a cinch to figure them out and stop him. They'll never score."

Elbert relaxed his jaw. Never score, eh? He'd see to it that they did. He was going to get busy on that smart aleck right now. He hesitated for a moment. Was it right to listen in on their plans? It wasn't as if listening would give him the answer, Elbert decided. He'd still have to figure out the plays himself. He clamped his teeth shut and concentrated. The Sampson team was in a huddle. Elbert listened carefully. Then the action started again, and Coach watched through narrowed eyes.

"I think Sampson is planning a run around the right end," Elbert announced in a loud voice.

Scott perked up immediately. "By golly, I think you're right," he roared. He leaned toward Coach, touching his arm. "Elbert ought to be in there," he said.

Coach sat forward, not saying a word. He watched the game intently. Sampson played it just the way Elbert had predicted, and the Rivertown linesmen only stopped them from scoring again by ending the action in a pile-up.

"If I were a quarterback, I'd try . . ." Elbert began, but was silenced by Coach's upheld hand. Coach was signaling to the referee. The whistle blew calling time out.

Coach stood up and eyed Elbert. "You seem to know what the Sampson boys are up to." He appeared to be thinking aloud rather than addressing Elbert. "It's worth a try. Elbert," he said in a louder voice, "get your gear on — you're in the game. It's up to you now. Use that head of yours." Coach turned and signaled to Steve, who trotted off the field.

Elbert clapped on his helmet. He slipped in the mouth guard, but his teeth felt tight and cramped. Taking the guard out, he clicked his jaws violently together a few times. Suddenly he stopped. Something had made a cracking noise. Quickly his tongue sought his special tooth, and then he spit something out into his hand. He stood staring at a piece of his filling. His finger went up to the spot. The filling wasn't all gone, but the top surface, the contact point, had chipped off!

There was nothing that Elbert could do about it now. Squaring his shoulders, he began jogging up and down the sidelines to warm up. In the background he could hear the excitement in the crowd. Sampson was being cheered again, while his own team received only an occasional yell. Then all at once he was out on the field running toward his team, and he forgot about everything else. There wasn't much time left to play, and Elbert knew that he had to act quickly.

Sampson was in possession of the ball. The teams took their positions. The ball snapped back from center, was received; the quarterback took it and began to run. Elbert tightened his jaw and listened hard. He tilted his head and concentrated. Nothing was coming in — nothing at all. Elbert wiggled his jaw. Nothing. And then he realized why. It was the mouth guard. If he wore it, his teeth couldn't touch, and then he couldn't receive any waves.

Elbert's first thought was to rip the darn appliance out of his mouth, but he knew that if he did he wouldn't be allowed to play at all. Still, he was mad — more at himself than anything else. Why hadn't he anticipated that the mouth guard would interfere with his reception? He didn't have any time to brood about it, though. The Sampson quarterback was attempting an end run, and in no time at all the Rivertown boys were upon him.

The Sampson boy fumbled, and Elbert found his feet moving as he raced to pick up the ball. Before Sampson had time to realize what was going on, the ball was firmly in Elbert's hands. He hugged it to his chest and ran as he had never run before toward Sampson's goal line. He could hear a field of players thundering down on him. He dodged one, gained a few yards, and then dodged another. His own teammates were doing a marvelous job of blocking, sacrificing themselves to get him through the Sampson territory. And then he realized that the sound that had been following him was getting farther and farther away, and he was aware that there was actually no one very near him.

Elbert mustered all the strength that he had left and sped down the field. At long last he stopped running and lowered the ball to the ground for the touchdown just as the whistle blew ending the game.

A sudden thunderlike burst greeted his ears as the crowd went wild. Elbert could hear his name being called out above the yelling and stamping of feet in the stands. He looked over at the scoreboard and watched the big 6 roll into place. The score stood 6 to 6.

Knowing that the try for the extra point would still be permitted. Elbert rejoined his team as they formed a huddle. Without any hesitation he called for a place-kick. As the teams reassembled, the boys could hear their schoolmates in the stands shouting:

Scalp 'em,
Beat 'em,
Get 'em,
Defeat 'em,
Get Sampson,
Get Sampson,
Go . . . go . . . GO!

Elbert called the signals. The center snapped the ball back to the holder; Elbert approached the ball and kicked. It was good, and the stands went wild again, whistling and stamping. Elbert's teammates were thumping him on the back as he watched the 7 to 6 roll up on the board.

He looked up to where his folks were sitting. His mother was waving a Rivertown banner wildly, and his father was standing on his seat cheering for all he was worth. Elbert felt like shouting himself.

He looked down at the ground and smiled, only

to be jolted by a hard wham on the back. It was Coach. His mouth was stretched in a smile from ear to ear.

"Great play, great play," he kept murmuring. "With a quarterback like you, Rivertown High will *really* go places!"

Elbert spit out the mouth guard and smiled. Then he tried working his jaw. He clamped down hard, but not a sound was coming through. Maybe losing the top of the filling had made it lower, he reasoned. He tilted his head and bit down harder. There wasn't even any static. It was gone — his magic was over. Cracking the filling must have ruined it.

Elbert pressed his lips together thoughtfully. Hearing other people's thoughts might be helpful, he guessed, but knowing that he could play football on his own without any "special" magic gave him a warm, comfortable feeling. He had done it all alone, and that was even better. But still he was sorry the magic was over. After all, it had gotten him into the game.

Slowly his hand went up to his mouth, and when no one was looking he rubbed his jaw fondly.